This book is dedicated to our KLF Kids - dream big, aim higher and work your hardest to achieve the greatness that is within you.

ISBN: 09893348-0-5
ISBN-13: 978-0-9893348-0-8
Library of Congress Control Number: 2013938803
AFE, LLC, Orlando, Florida

TOO TALL FOYLE
Finds His Game

Written by Adonal Foyle & Shiyana Valentine-Williams
Illustrated by Toni Pawlowsky

Far away in the middle of the shimmering Caribbean Sea,
Floats an island nation called **St. Vincent & the Grenadines.**

Like Hawaii, it is made up of lots of islands
And on one of the smallest lived a little boy. *Did I say little?*
Well maybe **not** so little...

He was as **tall** as a palm tree!
With incredibly **long** legs and arms,
Hands as **big** as coconuts,

And feet the size of his age...
a whopping 15!

In fact everything about him was so **big**
that the other kids called him **Too-Tall Foyle!**

6

Now Too-Tall Foyle **loved** to play sports...
but he couldn't find one that fit.

7

He **tried** to play soccer...
But he didn't like it when the other kids kicked the ball at him,
And instead of kicking the ball away,
he ducked and ran for cover!
So the other kids chanted **"Too-Tall Foyle can't play soccer!"**

And Too-Tall Foyle was **sad.**

He **tried** to play cricket...
But the ball was too small for his **big hands**
so he couldn't throw it right,
And he was **too tall**
to bend down low enough
to hit the ball!

So the other kids chanted
"Too-Tall Foyle can't play soccer or cricket!"

10

And Too-Tall Foyle was **very sad.**

He **tried** to run fast in a race...
But the distance was too far, And he ran out of breath before he could finish! So the other kids chanted,
"Too-Tall Foyle can't play soccer or cricket or run a race!"

And Too-Tall Foyle was really and **truly sad.**

But he loved sports and Too-Tall Foyle
knew that **he couldn't give up** just yet...

And then one day he heard about a new sport...
It was new to his island and not very well-known.
Too-Tall Foyle watched the other kids play from afar,

And slowly a **smile** appeared on his face...

This sport was **different**
from all the others
The court was smaller,
so his **extra-long legs**
could run back and forth
without getting tired,
The ball was bigger so his
huge hands could catch it
with the greatest of ease,

And the goal was a basket
so high up that the other
kids couldn't reach,
But, with a little leap,
Too-Tall knew he could!

Too-Tall Foyle **beamed...**

but this time he waited until all the other kids went home.

He grabbed the ball,
Ran down the court,
And **jumped up high...**

Soaring through the air, he stretched out **his extremely long arms** and *slam dunked the ball right down through the basket!*

18

Too-Tall Foyle had found his game.

And it was....BASKETBALL!

ABOUT THE AUTHOR

Adonal Foyle grew up in the tiny nation of St. Vincent & the Grenadines, where he first picked up a basketball at the age of 15. His quest for a college education which ultimately led him to the USA and into the NBA is an amazing and inspirational story of ambition, hard work and a little bit of luck.

The eighth overall NBA draft pick in 1997, Adonal played for a decade with the Golden State Warriors and three years with the Orlando Magic.

Adonal graduated magna cum laude from Colgate University and has a Masters in Sports Psychology from John F. Kennedy University. He is extremely active in the community and founded two non-profit organizations: Democracy Matters (www.democracymatters.org), a non-partisan campus-based project working to get big money out of politics and people in; and Kerosene Lamp Foundation (www.KLFkids.org) which uses basketball to engage and empower at-risk youth to grow into healthy and well-educated leaders in the Caribbean and USA. Adonal has received many honors, including induction into the World Sports Humanitarian Hall of Fame and the CoSIDA Academic All-America Hall of Fame.

www.AdonalFoyle.com

ABOUT KEROSENE LAMP FOUNDATION

Buying this book supports the kids of Kerosene Lamp Foundation!

Kerosene Lamp Foundation (KLF) was founded by NBA veteran, Adonal Foyle with the mission to empower youth to grow into healthy and well-educated leaders. Adonal named the foundation after the "Kerosene Lamp," the type of lighting he used to study by while growing up without electricity in the Caribbean. The Kerosene Lamp symbolizes his goal to light the path forward for today's youth. KLF uses basketball as a bridge to the next generation, promoting education (literacy) and health awareness through Athletics & Academics youth camps, mentorship programs, literacy initiatives and basketball court refurbishment. KLF is a 501©3 non-profit organization in the USA and St. Vincent & the Grenadines. Since inception, KLF has reached approximately 6000 kids in the USA & Caribbean. www.KLFkids.org

ABOUT THE AUTHOR

Shiyana Valentine-Williams is the Executive Director of Adonal Foyle's Kerosene Lamp Foundation. She is passionate about KLF's work to empower the next generation and throws her heart and soul into their youth programs.

Shiyana has been traveling to St. Vincent & the Grenadines for more than a decade and considers it a home away from home. A closet writer since a young age, this is her first literary undertaking. Shiyana received a BA in History and Peace Studies from Colgate University, and an MA in International Development from American University.

Ever since I was a little girl I loved to draw. I never outgrew that, and it became a passion. As a young woman, I began painting in watercolor for the pure joy of it.

After receiving an Associate Degree in Commercial Art in Madison, Wisconsin, I ventured out to Colorado where I worked at a newspaper, printing company, and a design firm.

I returned to Madison and family. My three beautiful sons are always an inspiration to me and I loved having children around me. Their open heartedness, innocence, and quick- to- laugh attitude with an abundance of energy, imagination and life made a wonderful world to live in. Illustrating children's books has always been a dream of mine. When I paint for children I can visit that world again.

Toni Pawlowsky

Look out for more _Too-Tall Foyle_ adventures coming soon!

For more information, visit www.AdonalFoyle.com or www.KLFkids.org.

Made in the USA
Charleston, SC
19 December 2014